LITTLE TIGER PRESS
1 The Coda Centre, 189 Munster Road,
London SW6 6AW
www.littletiger.co.uk

First published in Great Britain 2014
Text by Mara Alperin
Text copyright © Little Tiger Press 2014
Illustrations copyright © Ag Jatkowska 2014
Ag Jatkowska has asserted her right to be identified as
the illustrator of this work under the Copyright,
Designs and Patents Act, 1988
A CIP catalogue record for this book is
available from the British Library

ISBN 978-1-84895-658-2
Printed in China
LTP/1400/1008/1214
2 4 6 8 10 9 7 5 3

To Antoinette and Toby, with love ~ M A

For Michal and Eddie, who make my dreams
come true ~ A J

The Three Little Pigs

Mara Alperin

Illustrated by Ag Jatkowska

LITTLE TIGER PRESS
London

There were once three little pigs named **Horace**, **Boris** and **Percy**, who lived together in a teeny-tiny cottage in the forest.

One day Mummy Pig said, "You're all **too big** to live here, so you must go and build houses of your own. But beware of the **Big Bad Wolf** – take care your houses are safe and strong."

Big Bad Wolf

"Who's afraid of the **Big Bad Wolf**?"
chuckled **Horace**.
"Not me!" giggled **Boris**.

And so the three little pigs set off.
Before long, they reached a large field.

"I'll build my house right here
out of straw," Horace cheered.
"Straw? Are you sure?" asked Percy.
"Oh yes!" Horace said. "Then it's
playtime for me!"

And with a pat-pat-pat and a "Hip-hip-hey!" Horace built a house of straw.

Soon after, **Boris** and **Percy** reached the edge of the woods.

"I'll build my house right here out of sticks," **Boris** squealed excitedly. "Then I can go and play with **Horace**!"

"Sticks? Is that wise?" asked **Percy**.

"It's perfect!" **Boris** said. And with a stack-stack-stack and a "Tra-la-la!" **Boris** built a house of sticks.

All afternoon, Horace and Boris laughed and danced. They had quite forgotten their mother's warning.

Yippee!

But **Percy** plodded on. "I want **my** house to be safe
and strong!" he thought. Then he came to a brickyard.
"This is just what I need!" he said. So, day after day,
Percy worked with a *rumbley-bump…*

and a *tip-tip-tap…*

and a *heave-heave-ho…*

Until at last, his
brick house stood
tall and proud.

The summer passed. Then one day, Horace was taking a lovely, bubbly bath in his little, straw house, when he heard something growling. He peeped out of the window and saw two big, beady eyes.

"By my snout!" cried Horace. "It's the Big Bad Wolf!"

"Little pig, little pig, let me in!" bellowed the wolf.

"Not by the hairs on my chinny-chin-chin!" yelled Horace.

"Then I'll huff, and I'll puff and I'll BLOW your house down!" cried the wolf.

And he huffed.
And he puffed.
And whoosh!
Horace's house blew
down...
down...
DOWN!

Horace yelped and scurried all the way to Boris's house of sticks.

"Look out!" he cried, diving behind the sofa. There in the window were big, beady eyes and sharp, pointy claws. "It's the **B-b-big B-b-ad Wolf!**" Boris chattered.

"Little pigs, little pigs, let me in!" roared the wolf.

"N-n-not by the h-h-hairs on our chinny-chin-chins!" trembled Boris.

"Then I'll **huff**, and I'll **puff** and I'll **BLOW** your house **down!**" And so the wolf huffed. And he puffed.

And **crash!**

Boris's house clattered down... down... DOWN!

Horace and Boris squealed and galloped all the way to Percy's house of bricks.

"Look out!" they shouted. And Percy saw...

Big, beady eyes ...
sharp, pointy claws ...
and truly
terrible teeth!

"It's the
Big Bad Wolf!"
he cried.

"Little pigs, little pigs, let me in!"
howled the wolf.
"Not by the hairs on our
chinny-chin-chins!" shouted Percy.

"Then I'll huff, and I'll puff
and I'll BLOW your house down!"

And so the wolf huffed.
And he puffed.

And he huffed.

And he puffed.

But **Percy's** brick house stayed up … up … UP!

The **Big Bad Wolf** couldn't believe his whiskers! "I'm the **Big Bad Wolf**!" he howled. "**NO** tasty little pigs **ever** get away from **me!**"

"Oh help!" shivered **Horace**. "He's on the roof!"

"W-w-what shall we do?" asked **Boris**.

"Quick! I have an idea!" whispered **Percy**.

"Yum yum yum, here I come!" laughed the wolf, and he slid down the chimney...

...Right into
a **giant**
pot
of
boiling
water!

"OW! OW! OOOOOOOOOW!"

screamed the wolf, burning his bottom.

Then he leaped up
from the pot and
ran away as fast
as he could.

After that, the three little pigs never saw
the wolf again. And with help from **Percy**,
they built one big, strong house where they
could all live together.

My First Fairy Tales

are familiar, fun and friendly stories – with a marvellously modern twist!

The Elves and the Shoemaker

The Ugly Duckling

Pssst! coming soon!